The Spirit of Henry

Also available by Cristina Furtado:

The Story of Hope

This book is dedicated to my Momma. Her love, encouragement and friendship will always be paramount on my journey through life. I love you Momma!

I'd like to acknowledge my dad, Adolfo Quezada, once again for his help with editing this book and discussing his favorite thing in the world, hummingbirds. I love you Pop!

I was born to fly!

As early as I can remember, I wanted to fly. I wanted to soar and explore far away places. I wanted to feel the wind in my wings and freedom in flight.

I was born in beautiful Arizona along with my sister Hope. Our Momma built a cozy nest that kept us safe and warm until it was time to hatch. Hope hatched first, then it was my turn. I tapped the inside of my shell until it cracked open. Tap, tap, tap, CRACK! I shook away pieces of shell. I felt Hope by my side. Right away, Momma fed us our first meal. Her loving voice greeted us, "Hello my sweet babies; welcome to the world."

As soon as my eyes opened, I thought I could fly. After all, the big blue sky awaited me. "I think it's time Momma," I chirped. "Whoa, whoa whoa!" squeaked Momma. "You're not ready yet. You must grow a little and become stronger. I will teach you how to take flight, stay in the air, and land." "Okay Momma," I said, "but I'll be ready soon, right?" Momma sighed and said, "Be patient, son, you will be flying soon enough." Momma taught us many things about everyday life.

The day finally came when Momma told Hope and me that we were ready to venture out of our nest and each start our own journey in life. Hope had decided her journey would be fulfilled close to home. I chose migration, exploration and adventure. I promised to visit Momma and Hope between my travels and share my experiences with them.

The day I left was the hardest, and yet, the most exciting day of my life. "Here's to the start of my first adventure!" I thought to myself. As I flew away, I looked back to see Hope watching me. I knew Momma was also watching proudly from nearby. It was a warm summer day and the sun felt good on my back. I saw other birds heading south, so I headed in the same direction. I had decided that I needed to fly alone because I would be safer that way. It was all right to be alone because I knew that Momma, Hope and I were always together in spirit.

One day I followed other hummingbirds into a beautiful yard with a large red feeder and many beautiful flowers. I felt welcomed there. I drank from the feeder until my belly was full. I was so tired from all the flying and decided to take a nap. I found a small branch and locked my toes around it and fell into a deep sleep. When I finally awoke, I was hanging upside down. I sat up, laughed and said, "Oh dear, I hope nobody thought I was a bat."

As I soared over the vast desert, I saw saguaros, ocotillos, and a lot of wildflowers. I saw desert animals roaming the wilderness below me. I practiced all that Momma had taught me about gathering food safely, watching out for predators; and stopping from time to time for food and rest. Although I met many hummingbirds along the way, I continued to travel by myself.

Suddenly, something caught my eye. It was a hungry hawk looking for his daily meal. We locked eyes. "Oh no!" I gulped. He flew toward me with wings spread wide. I dove under him and darted away. He came after me again. I had to outsmart him so I flew backward, then under him and over him. I flew around him and made him feel dizzy. He shook his head, "You have a brave spirit little bird!" and flew away very disappointed.

As I continued on, I caught the smell of rain coming. A gentle rain started and the raindrops slid right off of my wings. "Ah, how refreshing." But the rain got heavier and the wind picked up, making it a challenge to fly.

I wasn't safe anymore so I took shelter and hunkered down safely under a bush. The storm blew all around me. The whistling of the wind lulled me to sleep. When I woke up the storm was over and I was safe. "That was kind of scary," I thought to myself. "Maybe I should head home." Then I remembered something Momma had told me, "You will face some difficulties but they are a part of your life journey. You will always get through them, and become stronger for it." I decided to continue on my journey.

I yawned, stretched, and came out from under the bush. I nourished myself with some little bugs; and I bathed in the rainwater that had collected in a fallen leaf. I scrubbed my belly and my back and shook myself dry. Then up and away I went into the big blue sky, onward to adventure.

I saw a beautiful park and stopped to rest. Two friends were enjoying a picnic. I hovered over them to get a closer look. One of them said, "Aw, look, a hummingbird!" The other one said, "They say that hummingbirds bring a spirit of good luck." I felt so inspired that I decided then and there that I would bring good luck to as many people as I could.

My travel had been far and wide and full of wonder, but now it was time to turn back home. I rested up under the night sky and reminisced about all that I had encountered on this adventure. I enjoyed my time away, but I missed Momma and Hope. I had so much to tell them!

When I finally arrived back home, Momma and Hope were excited to see me. I visited with them and shared my travel stories and adventure. They were so happy. They loved my stories and they loved me.

It felt so good to be home. But even before I had settled in, I had already made plans for my next adventure. I had chosen the best of two worlds: my journey in life would be filled with the thrill of adventure, and the love of my family.

Made in the USA
Columbia, SC
01 April 2025

55830003R00018